D0968474

Say "Hi!" Up High

Written by Dana Meachen Rau
Illustrated by Mike Dammer

Reading Advisers:

Gail Saunders-Smith, Ph.D., Reading Specialist

Dr. Linda D. Labbo, Department of Reading Education, College of Education, The University of Georgia

LEVEL A

A COMPASS POINT EARLY READER

For Charlie, who loves trampolines

A Note to Parents

As you share this book with your child, you are showing your new reader what reading looks like and sounds like. You can read to your child anywhere—in a special area in your home, at the library, on the bus, or in the car. Your child will associate reading with the pleasure of being with you.

This book will introduce your young reader to many of the basic concepts, skills, and vocabulary necessary for successful reading. Talk through the details in each picture before you read. Then read the book to your child. As you read, point to each word, stopping to talk about what the words mean and the pictures show. Your child will begin to link the sounds of the letters with the look of the words that you and he or she read.

After your child is familiar with the story, let him or her read the story alone. Be careful to let the young reader make mistakes and correct them on his or her own. Be sure to praise the young reader's abilities. And, above all, have fun.

Gail Saunders-Smith, Ph.D.
Reading Specialist

Consulting editor: Rebecca McEwen

Compass Point Books
3722 West 50th Street, #115
Minneapolis, MN 55410

Visit Compass Point Books on the Internet at *www.compasspointbooks.com* or e-mail your request to *custserv@compasspointbooks.com*

Library of Congress Cataloging-in-Publication Data
Rau, Dana Meachen.
Say "Hi!" up high / written by Dana Meachen Rau ; illustrated by Mike Dammer.
p. cm. — (Compass Point early reader)
"Level A."
Summary: A child jumps high, as a bird, a kite, and more pass by.
ISBN 0-7565-0176-8 (hardcover)
[1. Jumping—Fiction. 2. Stories in rhyme.] I. Dammer, Mike, ill. II. Title. III. Series.
PZ8.3.R232 Say 2002
[E]—dc21 2001004725

Printed in the United States of America.

In the sky
things go by.

A ladybug.

A bird with wings.

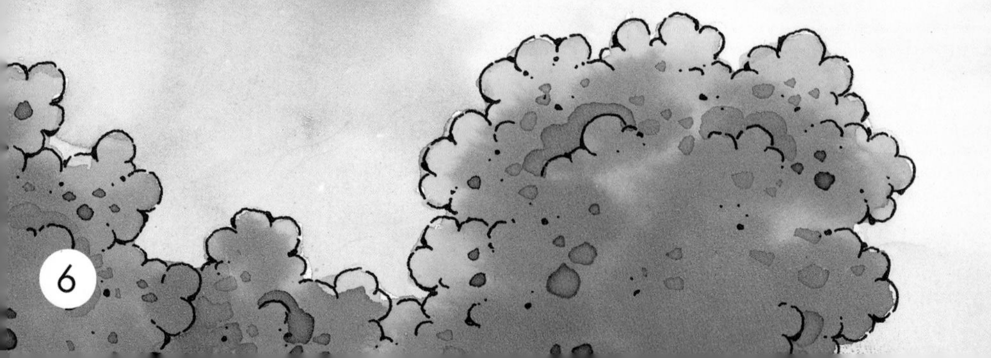

Some clouds that look
like lots of things.

When I fly
I say "hi!"

How can I fly
up in the sky?

A red balloon.
A purple kite.

A falling leaf.

A plane in flight.

When I fly
I say "hi!"

How can I fly?
I jump up high!

Word List

(In this book: 36 words)

a
balloon
bird
by
can
clouds
falling
flight
fly
go
hi
high
how
I
in
jump
kite
ladybug
leaf
like
look
lots
of
plane
purple
red
say
sky
some
that
the
things
up
when
wings
with

About the Author
When Dana Rau isn't in her office writing children's books, she goes for walks in her neighborhood in Farmington, Connecticut. She loves looking up at the sky while she strolls. She lives near an airport, so there are always lots of planes whizzing past. She also watches birds, bugs, and falling maple seeds. Someday, she hopes to watch a space shuttle launch into the sky.

About the Illustrator
Mike Dammer began his art career coloring on the walls of his parents' home in Chicago. After graduating from St. Xavier's College with a degree in business and fine arts, Mike got a job driving a bus. Soon he was hired by a greeting card company and his art career began. His favorite art medium is watercolor. Today, Mike lives in Tinley Park, Illinois, with his wife and three children.